W9-ALN-171

Thanksgiving
AT THE
Tappletons'

By Eileen Spinelli • Illustrated by Maryann Cocca-Leffler

J. B. Lippincott
New York

DISCARD

For Jer,
who made my wishbone wish
come true.
    E.S.

To my Uncle Dan, for his
encouragement.
    Love, Maryann

First published by Addison-Wesley Publishing Company
Thanksgiving at the Tappletons'
Text copyright © 1982 by Eileen Spinelli
Illustrations copyright © 1982 by Maryann Cocca-Leffler
All rights reserved. No part of this book may be
used or reproduced in any manner whatsoever without
written permission except in the case of brief quotations
embodied in critical articles and reviews.
Printed in
the United States of America. For information address
J.B. Lippincott Junior Books, 10 East 53rd Street,
New York, N.Y. 10022. Published simultaneously in
Canada by Fitzhenry & Whiteside Limited, Toronto.

Library of Congress Cataloging in Publication Data
Spinelli, Eileen.
    Thanksgiving at the Tappletons'.

    Summary: When calamity stalks every step of the
preparations for the Tappletons' Thanksgiving dinner,
they realize that there is more to Thanksgiving than
turkey and trimmings.
    1. Children's stories, American. [1. Thanksgiving
Day—Fiction] I. Cocca-Leffler, Maryann, 1958–   ill.
II. Title.
[PZ7.S7566Th 1985]   [E]   84-40793
ISBN 0-201-15892-2

Thanksgiving at the Tappletons was always a big day.

Thanksgiving at the Tappletons meant, of course, the Tappleton family:

Mr. Tappleton, Mrs. Tappleton, Jenny Tappleton, Kenny Tappleton

433551

WEST GEORGIA REGIONAL LIBRARY SYSTEM

And Grandmother and
Grandfather Tappleton
And Aunt Hetta and Uncle
Fritz And most certainly of
course. . .

The turkey and the
trimmings.

It was still dark when Mrs. Tappleton lit the oven and took the big turkey out of the refrigerator. Just then someone knocked at the kitchen door.

It was Mike the milkman.

"Good morning, Mrs. Tappleton. I thought you might like some eggnog for the holiday."

As Mrs. Tappleton reached for the eggnog, the turkey slipped from under her arm. Now, on a warmer day this might not have been a problem. But this Thanksgiving Day was quite cold, and the step was covered with ice.

Before she or Mike could even think, the turkey had slithered into the yard.

"Get it!" shouted Mrs. Tappleton.

Mike reached out but the turkey skidded past him, through the gate, and into the street.

"Hurry!" screamed Mrs. Tappleton.

"STOP THAT TURKEY!"

The milkman chased the turkey. . .Mrs. Tappleton chased the milkman. . .

And the turkey slid down the hill into the pond.

Plop! Splash!
It bubbled out of sight.

When Mr. Tappleton came down to breakfast, he took a long sniff.

"I don't smell turkey," he said to his wife.

"Of course you don't smell turkey," she replied. "You have a cold."

"I don't have a cold," he insisted.

Mrs. Tappleton shook some
pepper in the air.
Her husband sneezed.

"See;" she said, "you *do* have
a cold."

After breakfast Mr. Tappleton put on his coat and scarf and hat and gloves.

"I'm going to the bakery to buy our pies."

Mrs. Tappleton handed him his boots.

"Wear these," she said. "I know for a fact it is quite slippery out today."

Simms' bakery was so crowded the line reached out onto the sidewalk.

Mr. Tappleton hated to wait in long lines. So he went to the diner for a cup of coffee.

By the time he got back, the long line was gone. . .and so were the pies.

No pumpkin. . .no mince. . .no rhubarb. . .nothing.

Mr. Tappleton was afraid to go home with nothing.

"Two boxes tied up with string, please," he said.

Mrs. Simms stared at him.

"You mean two *empty* boxes?"

"That's right."

"My, they feel light,"
remarked Mrs. Tappleton.

"Certainly they are light,"
retorted Mr. Tappleton.
"Mrs. Simms prides herself
on how light her pies are."

Mrs. Tappleton set the table. She called to her son.

"Kenny, you may make the salad. There's lettuce in the crisper, and carrots and radishes, too."

Kenny's face grew pale. Just yesterday he had emptied the crisper and fed all the vegetables to the rabbits in Mr. Butterworth's class.

How could he tell his mother? He couldn't.

So he covered the empty salad bowl with aluminum foil and stuck it in the back of the refrigerator.

When the others went to pick up the relatives at the train station, Jenny stayed behind to mash the potatoes. Every year this was her job. She loved it.

"This year," she thought, "I'll make them even better. I'll use the electric mixer."

Just as Jenny flicked on the switch the phone rang. It was her best friend, Nora. If there was one thing Jenny loved to do better than mash potatoes, it was talk. Jenny talked and talked and talked to Nora, and she might still be talking today had not a wet *glump* of something hit her on the back of the head.

She turned to see what it was. Splat! Another *glump* hit her in the face.

The mixer was going wild
and mashed potatoes were
flying everywhere.

Without even saying goodbye to Nora, Jenny hung up the phone, scrubbed her face, and wiped mashed potatoes from nearly everything in the kitchen. She finished just as the others came back.

Uncle Fritz patted his stomach. "I'm hungry," he said.

Grandfather Tappleton laughed. "I'm as hungry as an elephant."

Everyone sat down at the table. It was a Tappleton tradition for Grandmother to say the Thanksgiving prayer.

"As soon as the turkey is ready. . ." she smiled.

"I'm as hungry as *two* elephants," said Grandfather.

Mr. Tappleton went to the oven.
"I'll carve the turkey now."
He opened the oven door.

"THE TURKEY IS GONE!"

Mr. Tappleton searched on the table and under the table and in every kitchen cabinet. He looked in the sink and in the broom closet.

"I can't find the turkey anywhere."

Mrs. Tappleton took a deep breath. She told them how their fine turkey had slipped out the door and down the steps and across the yard and through the gate and down the street and—plop! splash!—into the pond.

"So much for the turkey," said Uncle Fritz, and his stomach rumbled a little louder.

"Never mind," said Aunt Hetta good-naturedly. "We'll fill up on the trimmings."

"I'll get the salad," Jenny announced. "Then Grandmother can say the prayer." Jenny set the bowl on the table and peeled off the aluminum foil.

Everyone stared at the salad that was not there.
"I fed the rabbits at school," confessed Kenny.

Uncle Fritz looked downright gloomy.

"So much for the salad." His stomach rumbled again.

"I'm as hungry as *three* elephants," sighed Grandfather.

Kenny jumped up. "We'll have Jenny's mashed potatoes." He brought the pot from the kitchen and lifted the lid.

"I was on the phone," said Jenny meekly, "and the mixer went wild."

"So much for the potatoes." Uncle Fritz's stomach rumbled even more.

"I'm as hungry as *four* elephants," Grandfather declared.

"The pies!" cried Mrs. Tappleton. "I'll get the pies."

"I'll say grace as soon as the pies are cut," smiled Grandmother.

Mrs. Tappleton brought in the boxes, set them down, and untied the string.

"You brought home two empty boxes!" She glared at Mr. Tappleton, who covered his ears.

"*Five* elephants!" groaned Grandfather.

The dining room was quiet. Everyone looked down at the empty table.

Uncle Fritz muttered something, but it could not be heard above the rumble of his stomach.

A tear rolled down Jenny's cheek.

"No Thanksgiving dinner," she sniffled.

"Nothing to say a prayer for," sighed Kenny.

Grandmother smiled.
"Of course there is
something.
There is more to
Thanksgiving than a turkey
and trimmings."

And then Grandmother
Tappleton asked everyone
to bow their heads and to
hold hands around the
dining room table.

And this is the Thanksgiving
prayer she said:

Turkeys come and
*   turkeys go*
And trimmings can be
*   lost, we know.*
But we're together,
That's what matters—
Not what's served upon
*   the platters.*
Amen.

"That was a wonderful prayer," said Aunt Hetta.

Mrs. Tappleton jumped up. "We have liverwurst and cheese in the refrigerator."

"I'll help fix the sandwiches," offered Mr. Tappleton.

Jenny wiped her tear away. "I'll get the pickles."

Kenny laughed. "I'll open a can of applesauce for dessert."

And so, the Tappletons had their Thanksgiving dinner after all.

Uncle Fritz's stomach stopped rumbling, and Grandfather Tappleton ate enough liverwurst to feed *six* elephants.

In fact, everyone had plenty to eat. But most of all, they had each other.